the juggling pug

by sean bryan

illustrations by tom murphy

arcade publishing / new york

Do you all

know the story

of the juggling pug?

He

started

off

juggling

just

for

a

hug.

His town became famous,

and folks grew quite smug.

postcards
PUG SOUVENIRS

“We’re the home of

THE WORLD’S ONLY JUGGLING PUG!

It's okay if sometimes he poops on the rug.

He's a giggling, wiggling, juggling pug!

We forgive him
for giving our
curtains
a tug,

and for
smashing
our plates and
destroying our mugs.

Well… that's just how he is," people said with a shrug,

“He’s a troublesome,

worrisome, juggle-some pug."

Then one day a girl stomped her foot and said,

"UUUGGGHHH!

I've had more than enough of this juggling pug.

My yard is a mess with the holes that he's dug.

And every last one of my sodas is chugged.

(burp)

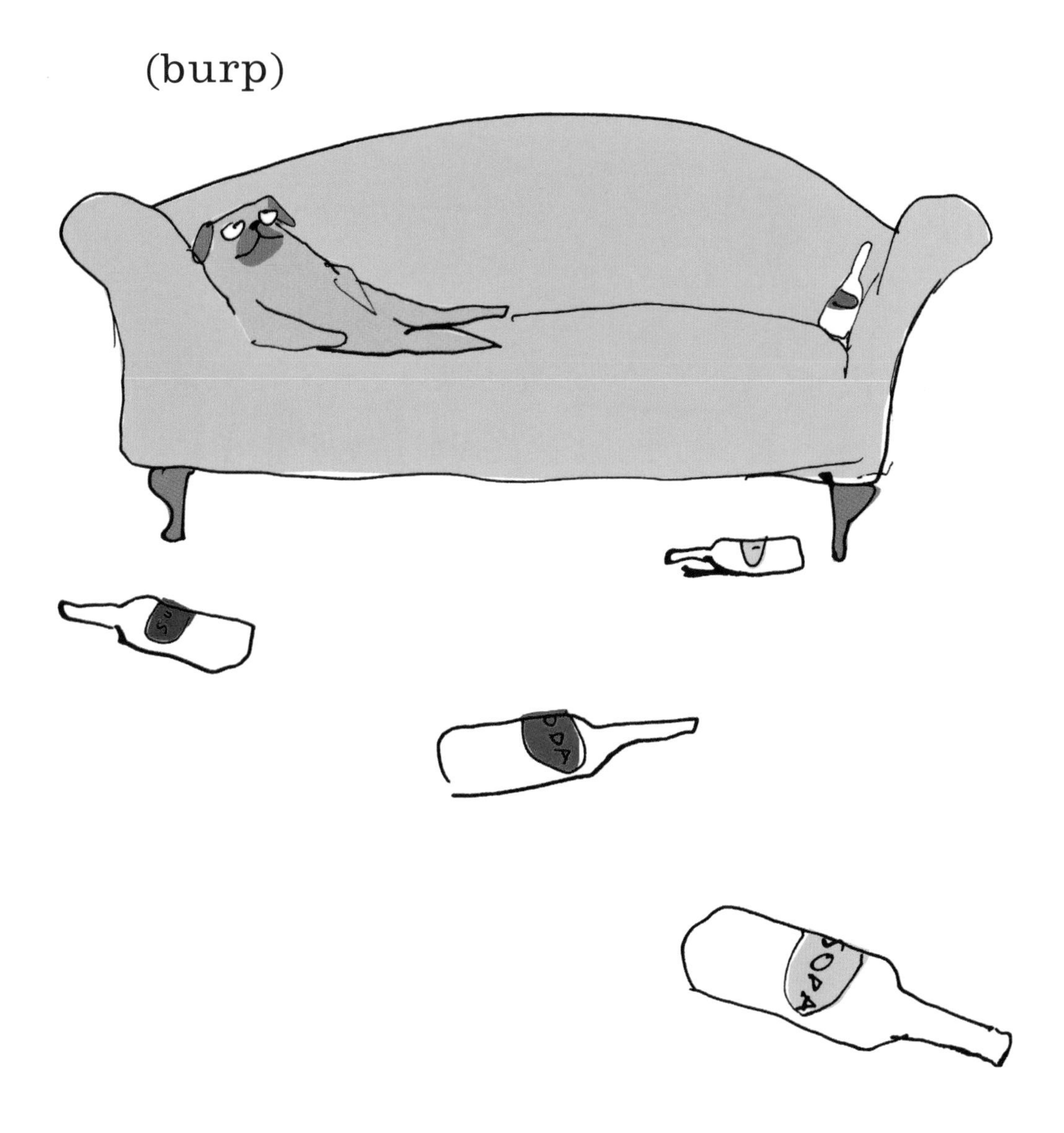

I don't care if he's famous,

I'm really bugged!

I say we get rid of that

juggling pug."

"No, wait, I can change!"

said the juggling pug.

"I won't act like a jerk,

I won't be such a lug.

I'll just snuggle and juggle.

C'mon guys, let's hug!"

So they did . . .
and the whole town
made up with the juggling pug.

Walking home,
he stopped off to see his friend Doug.

Nobody was home, so he pooped on the rug!

To Julia Rusk, and all the jugglers we've known:
Monty, Coco, Chloe, and Mugsy — SB

For Ellis, Sadie Grey, and Van — TM

FIRST EDITION

ISBN: 978-1-55970-874-6

Library of Congress Control Number: 2007035688

Library of Congress Cataloging-in-Publication information is available.

Published in the United States by Arcade Publishing, Inc., New York
Distributed by Hachette Book Group USA

Visit our Web site at www.arcadepub.com

2 4 6 8 10 9 7 5 3 1

Designed by Tom Murphy

IMAGO

Printed in China

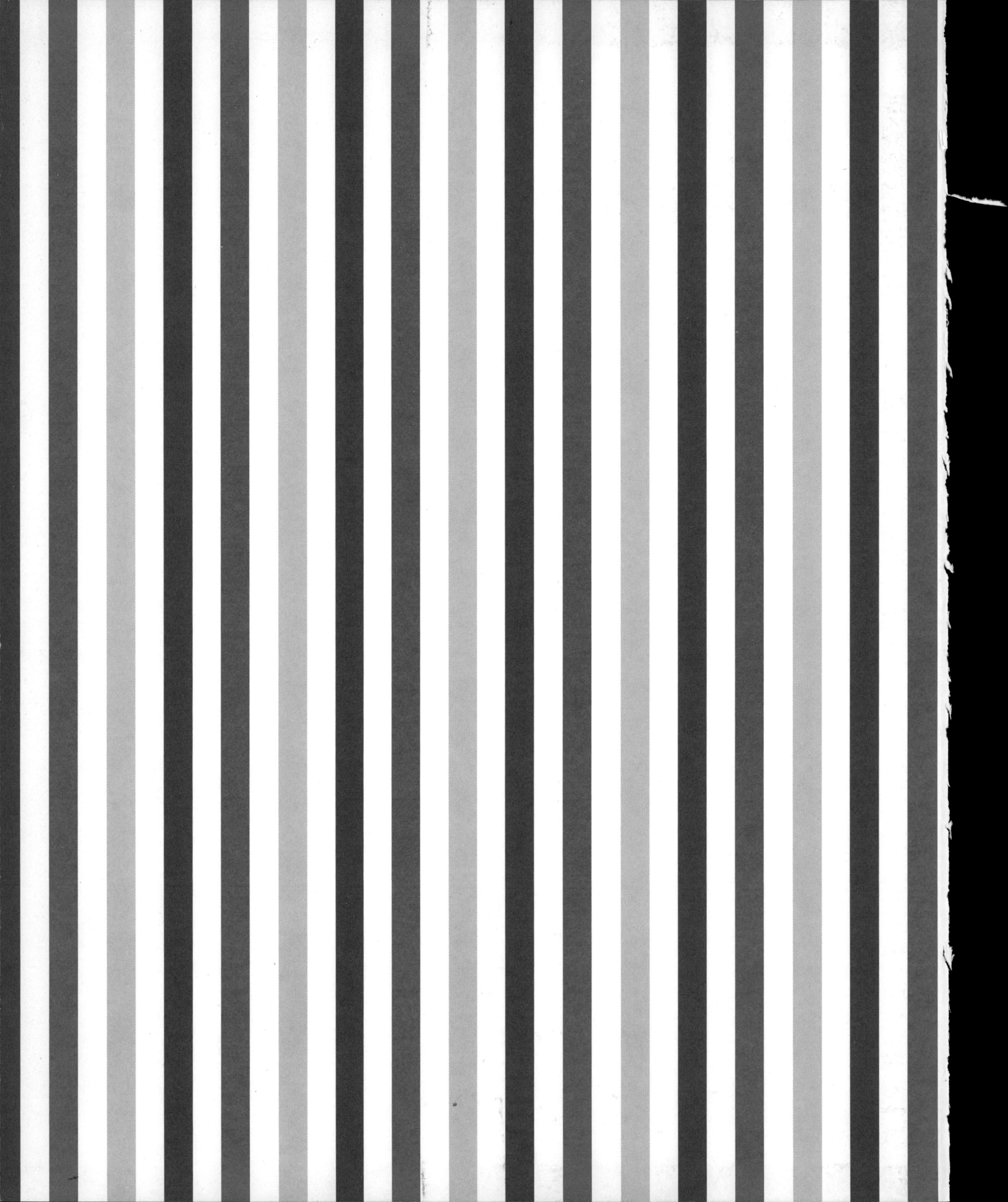